Beyond the Gilded Veil Love's Resilient Journey

"Beyond the Gilded Veil: Love's Unyielding Journey, Where Resilience Conquers Adversity and Perseverance Ignites the Soul."

suraj solanki

pencil

ISBN 978-93-5883-076-7
© suraj solanki 2023

Published in India 2023 by Pencil

A brand of
One Point Six Technologies Pvt. Ltd.
Unit no. 26, Ground Floor, Building A1,
Wadala Truck Terminal Road,
Near Post Office, Antop Hill, Mumbai - 400037
E connect@thepencilapp.com
W www.thepencilapp.com

Author biography

solanki

Solanki is a heartfelt storyteller, known for weaving emotional narratives that tug at the heartstrings. With a passion for capturing the essence of human emotions, Solanki's writing delves deep into the complexities of love, loss, and the resilience of the human spirit. From a young age, Solanki's love for literature ignited a desire to create stories that would resonate with others. As they grew older, their writing evolved into a powerful tool to express the depths of their own emotions and connect with readers on a profound level. With a background in psychology, Solanki infuses their stories with empathy and a deep understanding of the human psyche. Their characters come to life with raw vulnerability, leaving an indelible mark on readers' hearts. When not immersed in writing, Solanki finds solace in nature, drawing inspiration from the beauty of the world around them. Their contemplative walks often spark the beginnings of new tales, as they seek to understand the intricacies of human relationships and the transformative power of love."Solanki's writing evokes a rollercoaster of emotions, from heartwarming joy to poignant sorrow. Their ability to touch readers' hearts is truly exceptional," says one admirer of their work. With each story they pen, Solanki aims to remind us all of the beauty and fragility of the human experience. Their stories serve as a mirror, reflecting the myriad emotions that shape our lives and reminding us of the shared humanity that binds us all. As a writer, Solanki believes in the power of storytelling to heal and inspire. Through their words, they hope to leave an enduring impact on readers, offering comfort, hope, and a deeper understanding of the emotional tapestry that colors our lives.

CONTENTS

The Divide

In the bustling metropolis of Astoria, a stark contrast in lifestyles separated the affluent elite from the struggling working class. Among the privileged, Lily Kensington, the jewel of Astoria's high society, resided in a world adorned with opulence and extravagance. Born into immense wealth, her life seemed like a dream crafted by the gods of fortune.Her days were filled with exclusive galas, adorned with elegant gowns, and graced by the presence of influential figures. Lily was a vision of beauty and sophistication, captivating hearts with her grace and charm. She navigated the glittering social circles with ease, a symbol of prestige in a world where status and wealth held sway.Across the city's divide, in the shadows of gleaming skyscrapers, lived Aiden Sullivan, a tenacious soul who had known the harsh realities of life from an early age. Raised in a humble neighborhood by a hardworking single mother, Aiden's days were filled with endless challenges and responsibilities. The towering buildings surrounding him were not monuments of luxury, but reminders of the unyielding pursuit of survival.Yet, his spirit remained unyielding, determined to carve a path of success despite the odds stacked against him. He was a man of talent and ambition, gifted with a profound passion for art. Aiden's paintbrush became his solace, his canvas a realm where dreams and emotions intertwined.In the vibrant tapestry of

Astoria, Lily and Aiden were worlds apart, their lives seemingly bound to follow divergent paths. But fate, with its enigmatic hand, wove their destinies together in the most unexpected of ways.On a fateful evening, beneath the flickering lights of a charity gala, Lily's eyes met Aiden's across the crowded room. It was a moment that defied explanation, a spark that set the wheels of destiny into motion. From that instant, their worlds collided, and the boundaries between privilege and struggle blurred.In each other's presence, Lily found herself captivated by Aiden's unyielding spirit, drawn to the depths of his artistry and the authenticity of his heart. And for Aiden, Lily was a revelation, a muse who breathed life into his canvases and ignited a fire within his soul.But as their love blossomed in the midst of an unforgiving world, the chasm between their backgrounds threatened to tear them apart. Society's prejudices and family expectations cast a shadow over their budding romance, challenging the resilience of their hearts.As the metropolis of Astoria buzzed with whispers and judgments, Lily and Aiden faced a tumultuous journey of love and self-discovery. Their paths intertwined in a dance of passion and adversity, leading them to confront the essence of true love.In a city where class and privilege seemed insurmountable barriers, Lily and Aiden would embark on a courageous pursuit of happiness, defying expectations and daring to embrace a love that knew no boundaries.Their story was a testament to the enduring power of love, where the heart's longing transcends the confines of societal norms and elevates two souls beyond the gilded veil. In the grand tapestry of life, Lily and Aiden's love became a masterpiece, woven with the threads of passion, perseverance, and the indomitable spirit that thrives when two hearts beat as one.

Unlikely Encounters

Astoria, a city steeped in history and mystery, seemed to hold its breath as the intricate tapestry of destiny wove its threads that fateful evening. The grand chandeliers cast a soft, golden glow upon the opulent ballroom, adorned with intricate crystal ornaments that sparkled like stars on a moonlit night. The rhythmic waltz music enveloped the room, carrying an air of sophistication and elegance, as laughter and tinkling glasses filled the air. Aiden moved gracefully among the guests, his hands carrying trays of delectable delights, his demeanor a perfect balance of poise and unassuming charm. Little did anyone know that behind his discreet presence lay a world of untold dreams and aspirations. Aiden was an aspiring artist, his heart yearning to express the beauty he saw in the world through his paintings. Fate had led him to this charity gala, working as a waiter to support his artistic endeavors. Lily, on the other hand, embodied the very essence of the event's splendor. Dressed in an enchanting gown adorned with delicate lace and flowing silk, she seemed to float across the room like a celestial being. Her captivating aura drew admirers from every corner, but her heart remained untouched, for she sought a connection that transcended the superficiality of high society. When their eyes met, it was as if time suspended its relentless march forward. For a brief moment, the world around them blurred into insignificance, and the energy between them was palpable. Unbeknownst to the onlookers, the universe was orchestrating a cosmic dance, bringing two souls together in a mesmerizing tango. As Aiden and Lily exchanged glances, they felt an inexplicable familiarity, as if they had known each other for another lifetime. The depths of Aiden's eyes held the wisdom of an old soul, a profound understanding that resonated with Lily's sensitive heart. She saw in him a rawness, an authenticity that was rare amidst the polished facade of high society. Drawn to the authenticity and vulnerability in each other, they ventured to approach one another. In the soft-spoken exchange of words, they discovered shared passions and dreams, secrets whispered amid a bustling ballroom. They laughed at the irony of fate, the universe weaving their lives together in a place of grandeur and extravagance. As the night wore on, they found themselves dancing, their steps in perfect harmony, as if the music played solely for them. They lost themselves in the enchantment of the evening, surrounded by the grandeur of the gala yet cocooned in a world of their own making. From that moment on, Aiden and Lily became inseparable, their hearts entwined like vines on a trellis. They explored the streets of Astoria, hand in hand, finding inspiration in the city's hidden nooks and crannies. Aiden's paintings flourished with newfound passion, each stroke of his brush reflecting the love he felt for Lily, while Lily's artistic soul found solace in Aiden's embrace, basking in the serenity of his genuine affection. Astoria, once a city of strangers, now became a sanctuary for their love. The tapestry of their lives, once separate, now melded into a masterpiece of love and destiny. As their story spread like whispered secrets throughout the city, Astoria couldn't help but marvel at how the universe had conspired to bring two souls together in love so profound and extraordinary. And so, amidst the splendor of Astoria's lavish galas and the cream of society, Aiden and Lily found their forever within each other's hearts. Their love, a shining beacon of authenticity, proved that in the grand design of fate, the most unexpected encounters could lead to the most extraordinary love stories.

The Charade of Love

As the seasons changed, Lily and Aiden's love continued to bloom like the most exquisite flower, despite the challenges they faced. The moon became their faithful witness, shining down on stolen moments of tenderness and stolen glances that spoke volumes of unspoken affection. Their souls had found their perfect complement, their hearts beating as one in the symphony of fate. Lily's life was an intricate tapestry of privilege and responsibility, woven together by generations of wealth and societal expectations. Her family's name held weight in the upper echelons of Astoria, and her future had been predetermined since birth. A union with someone from a similar background was expected, cementing alliances and securing the family's status in society. But love, the wild and untamable force that it is, cared not for such constraints. As days turned into nights, Lily found herself torn between her heart and the world that had raised her. The prospect of defying tradition, even for a love so profound, seemed insurmountable. The weight of expectations pressed heavily upon her, like chains shackling her spirit. The very love that set her soul ablaze now became a source of turmoil, as she grappled with the consequences of choosing her heart over her duty. Aiden, too, felt the burden of their star-crossed love. His world was a stark contrast to Lily's, filled with humble beginnings and dreams that soared beyond societal boundaries. His family, though rooted in love and support, could never hope to match the prestige of the Kensingtons. The chasm between their social standings seemed impassable, like a great divide threatening to tear them apart. Yet, in the stillness of the night, when the moon and stars shone brightest, Lily and Aiden sought solace in each other's arms. They spoke of dreams and hopes, of a world where love transcended all boundaries, where societal expectations held no sway. In those intimate moments, they could almost believe that their love was enough to conquer any obstacle. As the days turned into weeks, their charade of love grew more elaborate, concealing their affection from prying eyes. Their meetings were clandestine, hidden in the shadows of Astoria's enchanting gardens or during stolen walks along moonlit cobblestone streets. Every stolen moment was a treasure, etched into the depths of their hearts, a secret sanctuary for their love to flourish. However, the weight of their secret began to take its toll. The burden of living a double life, pretending to be nothing more than acquaintances in public, was a constant ache in their hearts. The world around them was oblivious to the intensity of their emotions, to the depth of their connection. The charade became an intricate dance, a balancing act between their love and the facade they presented to the world. One evening, as the moon soared high above the city, Lily and Aiden found themselves at a crossroads. The silvery light bathed them in its gentle glow as they stood beneath a canopy of stars. They realized that their love could no longer remain a charade; it deserved to be set free, unburdened by pretense and secrecy. With trembling hands and beating hearts, they made a pact to face the world together, defy expectations, and choose love over tradition. They knew the path ahead would not be easy, that obstacles would arise, and storms might threaten to engulf them. But they were willing to brave the tempest, to walk hand in hand, hearts entwined, knowing that their love was a force of nature, unstoppable and unyielding. In the glow of the moon's radiant light, they vowed to fight for their love, to dismantle the barriers that society had erected. Their love story would become a testament to the resilience of the human spirit, a reminder that love could conquer all, even the most insurmountable odds. And so, with newfound determination and courage, Lily and Aiden embarked on a journey that would challenge their resolve, test their love, and redefine the boundaries of their world. For, in the end, they knew that their souls were meant to be entangled, and no force in the universe could dim the brightness of their love's eternal flame.

Love Tested

As the moon waxed and waned, so did the intensity of Lily and Aiden's love. Their hearts were entwined in a passionate embrace, but the world around them seemed intent on unraveling their once-seamless bond. The whispers of disapproval echoed in the corridors of high society, like venomous serpents hissing with malicious intent. Friends turned their backs, allies became adversaries, and the charm of Astoria's grandeur lost its luster in the face of judgment.For Lily, the weight of societal expectations bore down like an unrelenting storm. The disapproval of her family and the scornful glances of her so-called peers wore away at her resolve. She questioned whether the love she shared with Aiden could withstand the tempest of adversity. Doubt crept into her heart, mingling with the passion that still burned for him. The grandeur of her privileged life now seemed like a gilded cage, suffocating her spirit, and she yearned for the freedom to choose love over tradition.Aiden, too, felt the weight of the world's judgment pressing on his shoulders. He saw the doubt in Lily's eyes and felt the pull of her family's expectations tugging at her heartstrings. Insecurity gnawed at him like a persistent ache, and he wondered if he could ever be enough to stand beside her in the eyes of society. The echoes of disapproval reverberated in his mind, sowing seeds of doubt about the worthiness of Lily's hand.Amid the chaos, secrets, and lies emerged like cracks in a once-pristine facade. Family allegiances that had lain dormant for generations now stirred to life, twisting the truth and manipulating circumstances to fit their agendas. Long-buried rivalries surfaced, revealing a web of deception that threatened to ensnare Lily and Aiden in its clutches.As they tried to navigate the tumultuous waters, Lily and Aiden found themselves torn between their love for each other and the loyalty they felt towards their families. The fragile threads of their newfound love began to fray, and they struggled to hold on to the vision of a future they had once dreamt of together.In the face of adversity, they sought solace in each other's arms, finding strength and comfort in the sanctuary of their love. They vowed to confront the shadows that haunted their love story, to stand united against the storms that sought to tear them apart. But as the whispers grew louder and the disapproval more pronounced, they found themselves at a crossroads.Lily's heart ached with conflicting emotions, torn between her love for Aiden and the weight of her family's expectations. The path she had chosen once seemed clear, but now it meandered through a maze of uncertainty. Her heart longed for the freedom to follow her heart, but the fear of alienating her family and jeopardizing their legacy loomed over her like a dark cloud.Aiden, too, wrestled with his demons. He loved Lily with an unwavering devotion, willing to sacrifice everything to be with her. But the harsh judgment of the world threatened to shatter his confidence, leaving him feeling like an outsider in the world he longed to belong to.As the moon cast its glow upon their tear-stained faces, Lily and Aiden knew they had to confront the lies and deceit that surrounded them. They could no longer let the machinations of others dictate the course of their love story. It was time to rise above the shadows and stand tall in the face of adversity.With courage and determination, they set out to untangle the web of deception, seeking the truth amidst the maze of lies. As they unveiled the hidden truths, they discovered that the roots of their families' rivalry ran deeper than they had imagined. Old wounds, long forgotten, had fueled the animosity, and it was time to break the cycle of hatred that had shackled their families for generations.With honesty and vulnerability, Lily and Aiden confronted their families, laying bare the depths of their love and the toll the secrets had taken on their hearts. They pleaded for understanding, for the chance to forge a new path, one that transcended the feuds of the past and embraced a future of unity and love.It was a journey fraught with emotional turmoil, but in the end, the power of love prevailed. Hearts softened, old grudges were laid to rest, and the walls that had divided their families began to crumble. As the moon witnessed the reconciliation, it seemed to shine brighter, as if celebrating the triumph of love over hatred, of unity over division.Lily and Aiden emerged from the crucible of adversity stronger than ever before, their love fortified by the challenges they had faced together. The world that had once scorned them now bore witness to a love that defied the odds, a love that was authentic, unyielding, and unbreakable.As they walked hand in hand through the moonlit streets of Astoria, the silvery light danced upon their faces, illuminating the hope and determination in their eyes. They had overcome the darkest shadows, and now, together, they would face a future where love would be their guiding light, their anchor in the stormy seas of life.In the tale of Lily and Aiden, Astoria found a love story that would be whispered for generations to come, a testament to the power of love to conquer all obstacles and transform even the harshest of circumstances into a tapestry of beauty and resilience. And as the moon continued to watch over the city, it seemed to smile upon the lovers, knowing that their love had become an eternal beacon of hope in a world that so desperately needed it.

Struggling Against Fate

As the days turned into weeks and the weeks into months, Aiden and Lily's love story became a testament to perseverance and unwavering devotion. Despite the formidable odds stacked against them, they refused to succumb to the pressure and judgment that sought to tear them apart. Aiden's heart knew that his path to success as an artist would be a tumultuous journey, but he was willing to weather every storm, believing that love could bridge the seemingly insurmountable gulf between their worlds.For Lily, the struggle was equally intense, as her heart and mind waged a fierce battle. She had always been taught that her life was predetermined and that her duty was to fulfill the expectations of her family and society. But as her love for Aiden grew, so did her desire to break free from the gilded cage that had entrapped her. The dichotomy of her life became a constant whirlwind of emotions, pulling her in different directions, torn between the desire to follow her heart or conform to societal expectations.Aiden's determination knew no bounds. He worked tirelessly, pouring his heart and soul into his art, believing that one day his talent would shine bright enough to be recognized by the world. He knew that breaking into the art world, especially coming from humble beginnings, would be a daunting challenge, but he was driven by the love he felt for Lily, and he saw her as a beacon of inspiration, a muse that fueled his creativity and resolve.Lily, on the other hand, embarked on a journey of self-discovery. Her heart longed to be with Aiden, to experience a love so profound that it defied reason and tradition. She yearned for a life that was authentic, free from the constraints of societal expectations. As she explored her desires and dreams, she found the strength to assert her independence and confront the suffocating norms that had bound her.Their love story became a dance of compromise and understanding, where Aiden supported Lily's quest for independence, and Lily bolstered Aiden's artistic ambitions. They lifted each other, creating a powerful synergy that seemed to transcend the challenges they faced. They were determined to prove that love was not a weakness but a source of strength, a force that could overcome any adversity.As they navigated the stormy waters of societal disapproval, they sought solace in the small moments they stole together. Whether it was a stolen glance during a crowded social event or a secret rendezvous under the moonlit sky, every moment was cherished, every memory etched into the depths of their hearts. Their love grew stronger with each passing day, fortified by the trials they faced.Lily's family, initially unyielding in their opposition, slowly began to notice the change in their daughter. Her newfound independence and determination to follow her heart challenged their preconceived notions of her. As they witnessed the authenticity of her love for Aiden, cracks formed in the wall of disapproval, and seeds of understanding were sown.Meanwhile, Aiden's talent as an artist began to shine like the brightest star in the night sky. His paintings captured the essence of love, the beauty of Astoria, and the depth of emotion that only an artist in love could express. His work gained recognition among art enthusiasts, and his dedication to his craft became an inspiration to fellow aspiring artists.Their journeys of self-discovery and success intertwined with their love story, making it even more powerful and poignant. It was as if the universe conspired to align their paths, guiding them toward a future where love and dreams could coexist harmoniously.As time passed, the barriers that had once seemed insurmountable slowly crumbled. Society began to accept the love that blossomed between Aiden and Lily, realizing that love knew no boundaries, no social status, and no prejudices. The once-judgmental glances turned into looks of admiration for a love that had weathered the storms and emerged stronger than ever.In the end, Aiden's unwavering determination and Lily's burgeoning independence paved the way for a love story that transcended the confines of society. Their love became a beacon of hope for those who dared to defy norms, and who sought authentic love. Astoria, once a city of tradition and rules, now found itself touched by the magic of love's transformative power.And so, as the moon's silvery light continued to dance upon the stars, Aiden and Lily stood hand in hand, ready to face whatever the future held. Their love had weathered the trials of societal expectations and emerged victorious, a testament to the boundless possibilities that love could create when two souls found their perfect match. As they looked into each other's eyes, they knew that no matter what lay ahead, their love would always be the guiding light illuminating their path. Together, they were ready to embrace the world and create their destiny, a destiny entwined with the eternal threads of love and determination.

23

Betrayal and Redemption

As the moon continued to cast its silvery light upon the city of Astoria, it seemed to sense the storm brewing within the hearts of Lily and Aiden. Their love, once a beacon of hope and resilience, was now adrift in the tumultuous waters of unforeseen betrayals. For Aiden, the shadows of his past emerged like haunting specters, threatening to undo everything he had fought so hard to achieve. As whispers of his humble upbringing resurfaced, fueled by the malice of those who sought to destroy his newfound success, doubts gnawed at his resolve. He wondered if he was truly deserving of Lily's love, fearing that his past would forever taint their future together. The purity of his love for Lily became tainted by self-doubt, and he questioned whether he could ever be enough for her. Meanwhile, the very foundation of Lily's world crumbled beneath her feet as betrayals within her inner circle came to light. The very people she had trusted and confided in had conspired against her, using deceit as a weapon to manipulate her life and love. Her heart, once unwavering in its devotion to Aiden, was now burdened with the weight of disillusionment. The trust that had once bound them together faltered, leaving her questioning the authenticity of every memory they had shared. Amid these trials, Lily was faced with a choice that tore at her soul. Her loyalty to her family was deeply ingrained, and the disapproval she faced from them for her love for Aiden ignited an internal battle. She struggled to reconcile her desire for freedom and authenticity with her duty to uphold the legacy of her family. The very core of her identity seemed to splinter into conflicting pieces, leaving her feeling lost and torn. Aiden, too, confronted his demons, seeking solace in his art amidst the chaos. As he painted with brush strokes laden with emotion, he used his art as a cathartic release, expressing the turmoil that churned within him. Each stroke was a testament to his resilience, a way of showing the world and himself that he would not be defined by his past. But the pain lingered, and he knew that confronting his demons would be a necessary step in healing his wounded heart. In the darkest hours of their love, when it seemed as though all hope had been extinguished, Aiden and Lily were faced with a choice - to succumb to the shadows that threatened to consume them or to confront their demons and find strength in their vulnerability. It was during this time of darkness that Lily and Aiden realized the depth of their love, for it was in their brokenness that they found solace in each other's arms. They laid bare their fears and insecurities, confronting the painful truths that threatened to pull them apart. As they stood together, vulnerable and raw, they found a strength within themselves and in each other that they had never known before. They chose to face the demons together, supporting one another as they rebuilt the shattered pieces of their love. Aiden discovered that his past did not define him and that Lily loved him not for his background, but for the person he was and the love he had given her. Lily, in turn, realized that her loyalty to her family need not come at the expense of her happiness and authenticity. She found the courage to stand up for her love, unapologetically embracing her choice. The journey to healing their love was not without its challenges, but with each step, they strengthened the bond that had once seemed unbreakable. Forgiveness and understanding became the cornerstones of their love story, and the trust they had lost slowly began to rebuild, stronger than ever. As the moon continued to cast its silvery light upon the city of Astoria, Aiden, and Lily emerged from the depths of darkness, hand in hand, ready to face whatever the future held. Their love, though scarred and weathered, had been tempered by the fires of adversity, becoming a love that was both fragile and unyielding. They had confronted the demons within themselves and in each other, and in doing so, they had emerged as a love that was wiser, more resilient, and more authentic than ever before. Together, they knew they could face whatever challenges lay ahead, for they had learned that love, even in its darkest hours, could be a force of healing and transformation. As they walked into the moonlit night, their love story became a testament to the power of facing one's demons, choosing love over fear, and embracing the vulnerability that comes with true intimacy.In the end, the moon smiled upon them, knowing that they had found the strength to confront their shadows and emerge as a love that was as radiant and enduring as its silvery light. As they gazed into each other's eyes, they knew that their love, once tested and tried, was now bound by a bond that could withstand any storm and that together, they were ready to face the future, hand in hand, hearts entwined in a love that had been forged in the fires of their vulnerability and courage.

The Journey Within

As the dust settled from the storms of their love, Lily and Aiden found themselves at the crossroads of self-discovery. The trials they had faced had stripped away the facades they once wore, revealing the raw and vulnerable beings beneath. They realized that their journey of love had been as much about finding themselves as it had been about finding each other. For Aiden, art became both his refuge and his compass. Rediscovering his passion for painting, he poured his heart and soul onto the canvas, expressing emotions that words could not convey. The strokes of his brush became a testament to the power of love's resilience and the depth of human emotion. Each painting was a reflection of his journey with Lily - the highs and lows, the moments of joy and pain, the vulnerability and strength that love had revealed in him. Through his art, Aiden found healing and purpose. He embraced the vulnerability that had once scared him, recognizing that it was through embracing his own emotions that he could create something truly meaningful. Art became not just a means of creative expression but also a way to connect with others on a deeper level. As his paintings resonated with viewers, he understood that love, in all its complexities, was a universal language that could touch the hearts of strangers and forge connections beyond societal boundaries. Meanwhile, Lily's journey of self-discovery led her to confront the fears and insecurities that had once held her captive. As she delved into the depths of her soul, she questioned the values she had been raised with and the expectations that had been imposed upon her. She realized that her desire to break free from societal norms was not a rebellion but a quest for authenticity and freedom. In the process, she found an unyielding determination to carve her path, to live life on her terms. She faced the disapproval of her family with newfound strength, knowing that the love she shared with Aiden was worth fighting for. She understood that her happiness did not hinge on conforming to others' expectations, but on embracing her true desires and passions. Lily's journey of self-discovery also revealed a wellspring of compassion and empathy within her. She saw the world through a new lens, one that was more accepting and open-minded. As she learned to love and accept herself, she extended the same kindness to others, breaking down barriers and forging connections with people from all walks of life. Through their journeys, Aiden and Lily grew in profound ways. They learned that love was not a destination but a journey, one that required constant introspection and growth. They discovered that vulnerability was not a weakness, but a source of strength that allowed them to connect and the world more profoundly. As their paths converged once again, Lily and Aiden found themselves transformed by their experiences. Their love, once a fairy tale romance, had matured into a profound connection. They understood that love was not about perfection but about acceptance, not about smooth sailing but about weathering storms together. They stood hand in hand, ready to face the world as their authentic selves. Their love had weathered the trials and tribulations, and they had emerged stronger, wiser, and more determined than ever before. Together, they were a force to be reckoned with - two souls bound by a love that defied societal norms, a love that had been forged in the fires of vulnerability and courage. As the moon cast its silvery light upon the city of Astoria, it seemed to smile upon Lily and Aiden, knowing that their journeys had led them back to each other, stronger and more ready to face whatever lay ahead. Their love story had transcended the confines of tradition, becoming a beacon of hope for others who dared to follow their hearts and embrace their true selves. In the end, as they walked into the moonlit night, they knew that their love would continue to be a journey, a never-ending exploration of themselves and each other. And they embraced the adventure with open hearts, knowing that as long as they had each other, they could face anything that life threw their way, hand in hand, hearts entwined in a love that had been forged through self-discovery, resilience, and the unwavering belief in the power of their love.

Love's Triumph

As the sun began to set on their tumultuous love story, Lily and Aiden found themselves standing at the precipice of a new beginning. They had emerged from their odysseys stronger and wiser, their love now tempered by the fires of adversity and self-discovery. With newfound clarity, they realized that true love could not be confined by social status or material wealth. It was a force that transcended the boundaries of society, a flame that burned with eternal brightness.In a climactic moment that would forever be etched in the annals of Astoria's history, Lily stood before her family and the high society that had once defined her. Her heart pounded with a mix of fear and determination, but she knew that she could no longer deny the truth that had become the core of her being. With a resolute voice, she proclaimed her love for Aiden, unapologetically and without reservation.The room fell into stunned silence as her words hung in the air, their impact reverberating through the grand ballroom. Lily's declaration shattered the illusions of conformity that had once held her captive, and at that moment, she set herself free from the chains of societal expectations. Her love for Aiden had transformed her, and she was no longer willing to live a life dictated by others.For Aiden, Lily's declaration of love was a dream come true, one he had never dared to imagine possible. He stood beside her, his heart brimming with love and pride for the woman who had chosen him above all else. He understood now that true love was not about the trappings of wealth or social standing but about finding a soulmate who understood and cherished the essence of one's being.At that moment, Aiden's paintings, once expressions of his emotions and struggles, became testaments to the power of love's resilience. His art now embodied the beauty and authenticity of their love, transcending the boundaries of time and societal norms. Each stroke of the brush was imbued with the depth of his emotions, a reflection of the profound connection he shared with Lily.The room slowly came alive with a symphony of emotions. Whispers turned into murmurs, murmurs into applause, and applause into a standing ovation. The high society that had once scorned their love now bore witness to the triumph of love over convention. Lily and Aiden had shattered the glass ceiling that had confined them, proving that true love knew no boundaries and that the heart could defy all odds.As the echoes of their declaration resounded through Astoria, Lily, and Aiden knew that their love story had become a legend, a tale of hope and inspiration for all those who dared to dream beyond the confines of their circumstances. Their triumph over adversity and societal barriers became a testament to the indomitable power of love.Epilogue: Love's Eternal FlameBeyond the gilded veil of wealth and social status, Lily and Aiden forged a love that was timeless and boundless. Their journey had not been a fairytale but a story of resilience, growth, and the unyielding power of love. Together, they walked hand in hand, creating a life that transcended societal expectations and material wealth.Their love became a beacon of hope for those who dared to dream beyond the confines of their circumstances. They became advocates for the belief that love should be celebrated in all its forms, regardless of social standing or background. Their actions inspired others to reevaluate their perceptions of love, breaking down barriers and creating a more inclusive and accepting society.As the sun dipped below the horizon, casting its golden glow upon the city they called home, Lily and Aiden reveled in the warmth of each other's embrace. In the embrace of love's eternal flame, they vowed to cherish and protect their love, for it was a love that had defied all odds and emerged stronger than ever before.Their love story became a tapestry of courage and authenticity, a reminder that love, when nurtured and cherished, had the power to heal wounds and bridge divides. Lily and Aiden continued to grow together, supporting each other through life's challenges and celebrating each moment of joy. They knew that their love was not just a fleeting spark but a flame that burned brightly, guiding their hearts through the darkness and illuminating their path.In the city of Astoria, their love story became the stuff of legends, whispered by lovers and dreamers alike. It was a reminder that love was not about conforming to societal norms but about embracing the true essence of one's heart and soul. Through their journey, they had shown the world that the heart knows no boundaries, that love's eternal flame could conquer all obstacles, and that the power of love could transform lives in the most profound ways.As they walked into the moonlit night, their hands entwined, their hearts filled with gratitude, Lily and Aiden knew that their love was a gift, a treasure they would cherish for all eternity. And so, their love story continued a journey of growth, resilience, and unwavering belief in the indomitable power of love. Together, they would face whatever the future held, knowing that as long as they had each other, their love would continue to burn brightly, forever casting its warm glow upon the city they called home - the city of love, hope, and endless possibilities - Astoria.

Embracing New Beginnings

As Lily and Aiden stood at the precipice of a new chapter in their lives, they could hardly believe the grandeur of their love story. Their journey had been filled with twists and turns, trials and triumphs, but through it all, their love had remained steadfast and unwavering. The city of Astoria whispered their names with awe and admiration, for their love had transcended boundaries and touched the hearts of all who bore witness to its magnificence.As society's prejudices were cast aside, Lily's family was faced with the inevitable truth - that love knows no boundaries and that Aiden's worth was not measured by his financial standing. The once-frosty relationships thawed under the warmth of Lily and Aiden's unyielding love, and hearts began to soften. The barriers that had once separated them from Aiden's world crumbled, replaced by newfound understanding and compassion.In a grand celebration that echoed throughout Astoria, the two families came together, bound not by blood but by the shared love for the couple who had taught them the power of love's transformative magic. Aiden's mother, who had once been a staunch defender of societal norms, welcomed Lily into their fold with open arms, recognizing the goodness in her heart and the depth of her love for her son.Amid this newfound acceptance, Aiden's determination to succeed in his artistic endeavors intensified. He threw himself into his work, honing his skills and passion, pouring his heart and soul into each brushstroke. The emotions he once struggled to express with words flowed freely onto the canvas, and his artistry blossomed into a reflection of his love for Lily and the depth of his soul.As word of Aiden's talent spread, galleries across the city and beyond clamored to showcase his masterpieces. His paintings became a captivating symphony of colors, emotions, and raw vulnerability. With each stroke, he bared his heart to the world, inviting others to experience the beauty and pain of his journey. Soon, art enthusiasts and collectors from around the world sought to own a piece of his work, and Aiden became a celebrated artist in his own right, leaving an indelible mark on the art world.Meanwhile, Lily discovered her true calling beyond the confines of her family's wealth. Her experiences with Aiden opened her eyes to the struggles faced by the less fortunate in Astoria and beyond. Driven by a newfound passion for philanthropy, she founded a charitable foundation to uplift the underprivileged and provide them with opportunities for education, healthcare, and a better future.Her dedication to making a difference inspired those around her, and together with Aiden, she became a driving force for positive change in their city. Their joint efforts to break down barriers and uplift their community touched countless lives, leaving behind a legacy of compassion and hope.As they embarked on their journeys of artistic and philanthropic pursuits, Lily and Aiden found themselves becoming a formidable team, their love serving as the driving force behind their shared dreams. They traveled the world, spreading messages of love, resilience, and hope, sharing their own love story as a beacon of inspiration for those who faced similar challenges.Their journey became more than just a personal love story; it became a symbol of the indomitable power of love to overcome adversity and transcend societal expectations. People from all walks of life found solace and inspiration in their tales, realizing that love could truly conquer all obstacles when nurtured with compassion, understanding, and unwavering belief.As they traveled together, they continued to grow individually and as a couple, exploring the depths of their souls and the beauty of the world. Their love was a constant source of joy and comfort, a sanctuary in a world that could sometimes be harsh and unforgiving.And so, their love story continued to unfold, each chapter marked by new adventures, triumphs, and challenges. But through it all, Lily and Aiden stood hand in hand, their hearts forever entwined in a love that had defied the odds and emerged stronger than ever before.As the sun set on another day in Astoria, casting its golden glow upon the city they called home, Lily and Aiden reveled in the warmth of each other's embrace. Their love, like an eternal flame, burned brightly, illuminating their path and guiding their hearts through the darkness.In their love, they had found the strength to overcome adversity, the courage to challenge societal norms, and the power to make a difference in the world. And as they looked into each other's eyes, they knew that their love story was not just a tale of romance; it was a testament to the boundless possibilities of love, the resilience of the human spirit, and the transformative power of compassion and understanding.Together, they were ready to face whatever the future held, knowing that as long as they had each other, their love would continue to burn brightly, forever casting its warm glow upon the city they called home - the city of love, hope, and endless possibilities - Astoria. And as the last pages of their tumultuous journey were written, they knew that their love story would continue to inspire generations to come, a timeless tale of love's triumph over all odds.

Forever Bound

In the annals of time, their love story became legendary, whispered in the hallowed halls of Astoria for generations to come. Lily and Aiden's journey, filled with heartache and triumph, had molded them into souls intertwined by destiny, forever bound in the tapestry of love.As their love bloomed like a rare flower, so did their pursuits. Lily, fueled by her passion for philanthropy, expanded her charitable foundation beyond the borders of Astoria. She embarked on missions across the globe, seeking to make a tangible difference in the lives of the less fortunate. Her unwavering dedication inspired people from all walks of life, and her foundation became a beacon of hope in a world often overshadowed by darkness.In far-flung corners of the world, Lily and her team worked tirelessly to provide access to education, healthcare, clean water, and other essentials to those in need. Their efforts touched the lives of countless individuals, transforming communities and sparking a ripple effect of positivity and empowerment. Where there was once despair, there was no hope; where there was once darkness, there was now light.Aiden's artistic brilliance flourished like a supernova. His paintings spoke volumes, telling stories of love, resilience, and the unyielding spirit of the human heart. Each stroke of his brush seemed to capture a piece of their love story, etching it into the hearts of those who beheld his art. His exhibitions drew crowds from far and wide, and his paintings adorned the walls of prestigious galleries and esteemed collectors.Through his art, Aiden continued to touch the hearts of many, offering solace to those who needed it most. He used his platform to raise awareness for social issues close to his heart, shedding light on matters often overlooked or forgotten. His paintings became not just a reflection of their love but also a mirror that revealed the beauty and complexity of the human experience.Together, Lily and Aiden were a formidable team, their love and individual achievements complementing each other like the notes of a symphony. They became ambassadors for change, using their positions to advocate for social justice, equality, and the betterment of the human condition. Their love served as a testament to the transformative power of compassion and understanding.As the years passed, the city of Astoria transformed in their wake. The divide between the rich and poor began to crumble, replaced by bridges of empathy and unity. Society began to recognize the folly of judging worth by material wealth, and the belief that true prosperity lay in the richness of the human spirit gained traction.In their twilight years, Lily and Aiden would sit together, their fingers intertwined like vines of ivy, reminiscing about their journey. The love that had started with an unlikely encounter had grown into a love that knew no bounds. They would recount the tale of their love with laughter and tears, cherishing the memories of a lifetime spent together.Their love had become a guiding light, illuminating the path for those who sought to transcend societal barriers. Couples from all walks of life would visit the places where Lily and Aiden had once stood, seeking inspiration from the love story that had defied all odds.In the city's park, beneath the shade of the tree where they first met, a statue immortalized their love. Aiden's hands held a brush, while Lily's fingers cradled a globe, symbolizing their contributions to art and philanthropy, respectively. Their gazes met, mirroring the love and understanding that had bound them together.As they drew their last breaths, their spirits soared beyond the realm of the mortal world, leaving behind a legacy of love that transcended time. The city they called home stood as a testament to their love, forever transformed by the profound impact they had on its soul.As the stars above twinkled in approval, Lily and Aiden found solace in the knowledge that their love had become a constellation in the universe, its light guiding the hearts of generations to come. Their love had transcended the boundaries of earthly existence, forever etched in the cosmos as a beacon of hope, unity, and the enduring power of love.Astoria continued to be their canvas, painted with the brushstrokes of their love and the colors of their legacy. Their love story would forever be whispered among the stars, a tale of two souls who defied the odds, shattered barriers, and left an indelible mark on the world with the transformative power of their love.In the hearts of those who knew them and those who would come to know their legend, Lily and Aiden's love would continue to blossom, inspiring generations to believe in the magic of love, the strength of resilience, and the potential of humanity to create a more compassionate and understanding world.And so, as time marched on, their love story would remain etched in the tapestry of history, a timeless reminder that true love knows no boundaries, transcends all obstacles and leaves an everlasting impression on the hearts of those who dare to dream and believe in the power of love's eternal flame.

A Heartbreaking Farewell

As the weight of societal expectations bore down upon Lily and Aiden's love, cracks began to appear in the once-unbreakable bond that had flourished like a rare and delicate flower. The vibrant colors of their world began to fade, replaced by shades of sorrow and uncertainty. A sense of impending doom seemed to hang over them like a dark cloud, threatening to shatter the love they had fought so hard to protect.Lily, torn between her heart and her family's disapproval, found herself trapped in a suffocating web of conflicting emotions. The walls of their love seemed to be closing in around her, leaving her feeling torn and unable to breathe. The once-clear path they had envisioned together now seemed hazy and uncertain. She felt torn between her love for Aiden and the life she had been born into, torn between the expectations placed upon her and the desires of her heart.Aiden, who had once been the embodiment of resilience, now felt his spirit waning as he faced the constant battles against the odds. The world seemed determined to keep him in the shadows, and the weight of the societal barriers that separated him from Lily became increasingly heavy to bear. Despite his determination to prove his worth, it felt as though every step forward was met with an invisible force pushing him back.In a heart-wrenching confrontation, Lily's family delivered an ultimatum, forcing her to face an impossible choice. She was torn between forsaking her love for Aiden and conforming to their expectations or defying them and risking being cast out from the only world she had ever known. The pressure to protect her family's legacy clashed with the deep-rooted love she held for Aiden, leaving her trapped in an emotional whirlwind.Torn between two worlds, Lily found herself standing at a crossroads, her heart aching with the weight of her decision. She knew that choosing Aiden would mean severing ties with her family and the world she had once embraced. The thought of losing them, of losing her place in the life she had known, tore at her heart. Yet, the thought of losing Aiden was equally unbearable.Aiden, sensing Lily's internal struggle, recognized the heaviness in her eyes. He understood the tremendous burden she carried and how their love had become a double-edged sword, cutting deep into their souls with every passing moment. As much as he wished to hold on to her and fight for their love, he also understood the complexity of the situation.With a heavy heart, Lily made her choice, and at that moment, their love story took an irreversible turn. She chose to protect her family's legacy and succumbed to the expectations placed upon her, breaking Aiden's heart and her own in the process. In a tearful goodbye, Lily and Aiden stood before each other, the unspoken words hanging heavily in the air. They both knew that their love was still burning fiercely, but the circumstances had conspired against them. As they embraced one last time, the city of Astoria seemed to mourn the tragic love that was slipping through their fingers. The skies wept with rain, mirroring the sorrow in their hearts. With a tearful gaze, Lily turned away from Aiden and walked away, leaving him shattered and desolate. As she retreated into her world of privilege, Aiden was left with a heart that would forever bear the scars of lost love. In the years that followed, they both tried to move on with their lives, but the void left by their love remained unfillable. Lily married a man of her family's choosing, as the weight of her decision settled heavily upon her shoulders. She tried to embrace her new life and fulfill her role in society, but the love she had once known continued to linger in the depths of her heart.Meanwhile, Aiden poured his heart and soul into his art, seeking solace and meaning in the canvas before him. But no matter how brilliant his paintings were, the colors on his canvas could never capture the vibrancy of the love he had once known. His art became a way to express the depths of his emotions and the ache of his heart.In the end, they both lived lives of silent longing, haunted by the ghost of a love that could never be. Their paths never crossed again, but their hearts remained forever entwined in the tragic tale of a love that had been destined to fall. As they moved through life, the memories of their time together lingered like a bittersweet melody, a constant reminder of what could have been.Their love story became a bittersweet legend, whispered by the city's streets and immortalized in the hearts of those who had witnessed its fleeting brilliance. In the heart of Astoria, beneath the tree where they had first met, a lone statue stood as a poignant reminder of the love that had once bloomed but was destined to wither away.The city of Astoria wept for the love that had been lost, and its tears mingled with the rain as a testament to a love that had been destined to remain forever unfulfilled. The tragedy of Lily and Aiden's love story became a cautionary tale, a reminder of the profound impact societal expectations could have on the course of love.In the end, their love story served as a poignant reminder that love, no matter how powerful, could sometimes succumb to the pressures of the world. Their love had been flame that burned brightly but was ultimately extinguished by the storm of expectations and circumstances.And so, the tale of Lily and Aiden's love became etched in the fabric of time, a timeless reminder of the complexities of love and the fragile nature of the human heart. As the city of Astoria continued to grow and change, the memory of their love would forever be held dear, a poignant and tragic tale of two souls who had once dared to defy the world for the sake of love.As the years passed and the echoes of their love story faded, the city of Astoria continued to evolve and transform. Yet, the memory of Lily and Aiden's love remained etched in the fabric of time, becoming a poignant reminder of the complexities of love and the fragile nature of the human heart.Astoria's society underwent a gradual shift, influenced by the profound impact of Lily and Aiden's tragic love story. The once-rigid boundaries between social classes began to soften as people began to question the societal norms that had once held them captive. The tale of Lily and Aiden's love left an indelible mark on the city's collective consciousness, inspiring conversations about the importance of empathy, compassion, and the power of following one's heart.Lily, burdened by the weight of her decision to choose societal expectations over love, lived a life that appeared perfect on the surface but was haunted by a deep sense of longing. Despite her position in high society, she often found herself feeling isolated and unfulfilled. The love she had once sacrificed continued to linger in the depths of her heart, serving as a constant reminder of what could have been.In the quiet moments of solitude, Lily would find herself gazing at the statue beneath the tree in the park, the monument to the love she had lost. It stood as a symbol of the path not taken, a constant reminder of the love that had once bloomed but was destined to wither away. Despite her role in the charitable foundation, Lily felt that she could never fill the void left by her lost love.Aiden, on the other hand, channeled his pain and heartache into his art, creating masterpieces that continued to resonate with audiences far and wide. His paintings captured the essence of love, loss, and resilience, and the emotions poured into each brushstroke were felt by all who beheld his work. He had become a renowned artist, but his heart was forever scarred by the memory of his lost love.Despite their divergent paths, both Lily and Aiden never forgot the love they had shared. The years only deepened the ache in their hearts, and they each found themselves grappling with the lingering question of "what if." As they grew older, the yearning to see each other once more intensified, but they remained apart, held back by the decisions they had made in the past.The city of Astoria, now a symbol of progress and unity, embraced the legacy of Lily and Aiden's love story. The once-divided city now stood as a testament to the transformative power of love and the ability to overcome societal barriers. The park where they had first met became a place of pilgrimage for couples seeking to find solace and guidance in their own love stories.The statue beneath the tree became a symbol of hope and a reminder of the fragility of love in the face of adversity. People from all walks of life would visit the monument, seeking inspiration and guidance from the love that had once burned so brightly. Lily and Aiden's love story served as a beacon of light, encouraging others to pursue their happiness, regardless of societal expectations.As the city evolved, so did its residents' perspectives on love and relationships. The once-judgmental eyes of society softened, replaced by understanding and acceptance. The divide between the rich and the less fortunate began to narrow as Lily's charitable foundation continued to make a significant impact on the lives of many.Aiden's artwork, which once struggled to gain recognition, now adorned the walls of museums and galleries around the world. His paintings continued to touch the hearts of those who viewed them, acting as a reminder of the power of love's endurance and the resilience of the human spirit.As their own love stories unfolded, young couples in Astoria would look to the tale of Lily and Aiden as an example of the challenges love might face and the importance of cherishing love above all else. Their love story became a lesson in the significance of choosing love over societal expectations, as well as the consequences of forsaking one's heart's true desires.In the twilight of their lives, Lily and Aiden both found themselves reflecting on the paths they had chosen. While life had taken them on separate journeys, the love they had once shared remained an integral part of their souls. Each yearning for closure, they each penned letters to one another, finally expressing the depths of their emotions that had remained unspoken for so long.In the final chapter of their love story, Lily and Aiden's letters found their way into each other's hands. The letters were filled with heartfelt confessions of love, regret, and longing. Their words served as a balm to the wounds of lost love, offering comfort and understanding in the knowledge that they had both cherished the memories of their time together.In a poignant twist of fate, Lily and Aiden found themselves standing once more beneath the tree where their love had first bloomed. The weight of the years seemed to fall away as they looked into each other's eyes, their souls recognizing the love that had never truly faded. They embraced, and at that moment, they both knew that their love had endured despite the passage of time and the choices they had made.In their reunion, the city of Astoria seemed to rejoice, for the love that had once been lost had found its way back home. Their love story, now complete, became a tale of redemption and forgiveness, proving that love's endurance could transcend the boundaries of time and societal expectations.In their embrace, Lily and Aiden finally found the closure they had sought for so long. They realized that their love had never truly died, but had instead evolved and matured with the passing years. Their paths may have diverged, but fate had led them back to each other, demonstrating that the bonds of love could never truly be broken.Their love story, once etched in the tapestry of tragedy, had now become a story of hope, resilience, and the power of second chances. The city of Astoria, forever changed by their love, celebrated their reunion as a symbol of the enduring nature of true love.As the sun set on their lives, Lily and Aiden stood hand in hand, their hearts forever intertwined in the love story that had defied all odds. Their legacy lived on, not just in the memory of the city they called home, but in the hearts of generations to come. The tale of Lily and Aiden's love had become a timeless reminder that love, even in the face of adversity, could find its way back to where it truly belonged - in the arms of the one who had always held the key to its eternal flame.

Love's Eternal Embrace

In the closing chapters of their love story, fate dealt an unexpected and tragic twist. Lily, who had lived a life of privilege and philanthropy, was suddenly faced with a terminal illness that defied all medical efforts to overcome. The news came as a devastating blow to her family, to Aiden, and to the entire city of Astoria, who had witnessed the extraordinary journey of their love. As Lily's health rapidly deteriorated, she found solace in the arms of Aiden, who never left her side. The love they had once shared only intensified in the face of the impending loss, and they clung to each other with the desperation of souls who knew they were running out of time. Aiden poured his heart and soul into creating a series of paintings that captured the essence of their love, the fleeting beauty of their time together, and the profound sorrow of their parting. Each brushstroke seemed to carry a piece of his heart, immortalizing their love on the canvas for eternity. In their final moments together, Lily and Aiden found strength in their shared memories, in the laughter they had shared, and in the dreams they had once dared to dream together. With tear-stained cheeks, they whispered promises of eternal love and the hope of meeting again someday. The city of Astoria stood in collective mourning as news of Lily's passing spread. She had been a beacon of light, not just as a philanthropist, but as a symbol of the transformative power of love. Her loss was felt deeply, not only by her family and friends but also by the countless lives she had touched through her charitable work. In the park beneath the tree where Lily and Aiden had first met, a somber atmosphere settled over the statue that immortalized their love. Astoria's citizens gathered to pay their respects, leaving flowers and messages of gratitude for the couple who had forever changed the city's heart. As the sun set on the day of Lily's funeral, Aiden found himself standing alone beneath the tree. He felt the weight of grief and the emptiness that comes from losing a soulmate. But he also knew that the love they had shared would forever live on in his heart and in the memories of those who had been touched by their story. In the years that followed, Aiden continued to create art that bore the imprint of Lily's presence. His paintings became a tribute to their love, capturing the bittersweet beauty of their time together and serving as a reminder of the fragility of life and the importance of cherishing the ones we love. Astoria, forever touched by the love story of Lily and Aiden, continued to celebrate their legacy. The park beneath the tree became a place of reflection and inspiration, where couples would come to seek guidance from the tale of love that had defied all odds. In the hearts of the city's residents, Lily's memory lived on as an enduring symbol of love's power to transcend boundaries and touch lives. The charitable foundation she had built continued to thrive, carrying on her mission of making a difference in the lives of others. As Aiden's life continued, he knew that his time on Earth would always be connected to Lily's. He found comfort in knowing that their love had been a force that had changed the trajectory of countless lives and had left an indelible mark on the city they called home. In the quiet moments of the evening, as the sun dipped below the horizon, Aiden would often visit the park, sitting beneath the tree where their love had first taken root. He would gaze at the statue, hand outstretched to touch the stone that bore Lily's likeness. In the breeze that rustled the leaves, Aiden would feel a whisper of her presence, and in the warmth of the sun's rays, he would find a glimmer of hope. He knew that though they were separated by the veil of mortality, their love had transcended the boundaries of time, etching itself into the very fabric of the universe. In the city of Astoria, the legend of Lily and Aiden's love story lived on, whispered in the hearts of its people, and carried in the winds that swept through its streets. Their love had become a constellation in the cosmos, its light guiding the hearts of generations to come, a testament to the enduring power of love that defies even death itself.